ALICE
in
WONDERLAND

LEVEL 5

Re-told by: Paul Shipton
Series Editor: Melanie Williams

Pearson Education Limited
Edinburgh Gate, Harlow,
Essex CM20 2JE, England
and Associated Companies throughout the world.

ISBN: 978-1-4082-8737-8

This edition first published by Pearson Education Ltd. 2013

1 3 5 7 9 10 8 6 4 2

Set in 15/19pt OT Fiendstar
Printed in China
SWTC/01

Published by Pearson Education Ltd. in association with
Penguin Books Ltd. both companies being subsidiaries of Pearson Plc.

For a complete list of the titles available in the Penguin Kids series please go to www.penguinreaders.com.
Alternatively, write to your local Pearson Education office or to: Penguin Readers Marketing Department,
Pearson Education, Edinburgh Gate, Harlow, Essex CM20 2JE, England.

It was a beautiful sunny afternoon. Alice sat on a tree near the river, but she could not close her eyes and dream. Her big sister wanted to read a book to her and Alice had to listen carefully.

"Alice!" said her sister.

"I'm listening," answered Alice. "But it's not easy to listen to a book with no pictures. In *my* world, all books have only pictures and no words."

In the world in Alice's mind, *everything* was different.

Suddenly, Alice heard a new voice.

"I'm late!" said the voice nervously. "I'm late, for a very important date!"

Something ran by. It was a white rabbit. He wore clothes and he held a big watch in one paw. "I'm late!" said the rabbit again.

"That's very strange!" said Alice to her little cat Dinah. "What is he late *for*? Perhaps it's something important. Perhaps it's a party!"

She started to run after the White Rabbit. "Mr. Rabbit!"

4

Alice came to a hole at the bottom of a tree.

"This is a strange place for a party," she said.

Alice wanted to know more about the rabbit, so she went into the hole on her hands and knees. Dinah tried to follow her.

Under the tree the hole became bigger and Alice fell. It was a long way down. But this was more exciting than that boring book!

"Goodbye, Dinah!" she shouted.

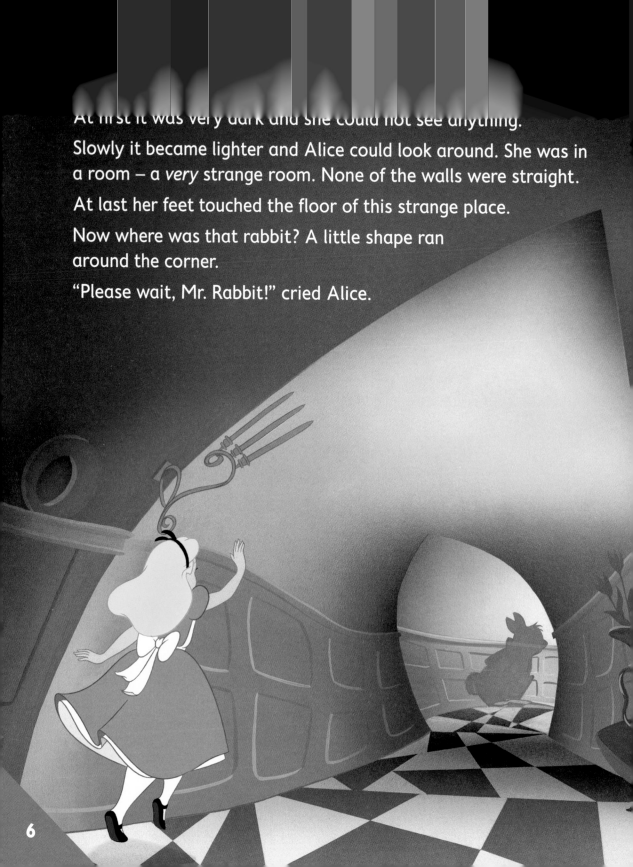

At first it was very dark and she could not see anything.

Slowly it became lighter and Alice could look around. She was in a room – a *very* strange room. None of the walls were straight.

At last her feet touched the floor of this strange place.

Now where was that rabbit? A little shape ran around the corner.

"Please wait, Mr. Rabbit!" cried Alice.

There was no rabbit around the corner, only a little door. Alice opened it and found a smaller door. Behind that there was a much smaller door. Behind *that* was the smallest door of all.

Alice had to go through the smallest door on her hands and knees. Now she was in another room, and there was another door with a gold doorknob.

Alice tried to open the door and the Doorknob cried, "OW!" Alice was very surprised. "I'm sorry!"

"You're too big for this door," said the Doorknob. "Try the bottle."

Suddenly, there was a table behind Alice. On the table there was a bottle with a label – DRINK ME.

Alice drank once, twice, three times. With each drink, she shrank. Soon she was smaller than the bottle!

"Now I can use the door," she said.

"Not without a key," laughed the Doorknob.

There was a key on the table, but little Alice could not reach it.

"Try the box," the Doorknob said.

Inside the box on the floor, Alice found a cookie with the words – EAT ME.

Alice bit the cookie and began to grow. Her head hit the ceiling. Now she was *much* too big.

Alice began to cry and cry. Soon there was a sea of tears in the room.

Alice quickly drank some more. She became smaller again and fell into the empty bottle.

Her tears carried the bottle through the keyhole.

On the other side of the door, Alice soon came to the end of the sea of tears. She was at a beach. She climbed out of the bottle and walked toward the forest of tall trees in front of her.

Then she arrived at a little house in the forest.

"Who lives here?" asked Alice.

She quickly learned the answer to her question. The door opened and the little White Rabbit ran out.

The rabbit pulled a watch from his pocket.

"What are you doing out here?" he cried at Alice. "I'm LATE! Go and get my gloves!" He pointed inside the house with one little white paw.

Alice went inside and began to look around. "Where do rabbits keep their gloves?"

She looked inside a little box. There were no gloves there, but there *was* another cookie with the words – EAT ME.

"All right," said Alice, and she ate the cookie.

Alice began to *grow*.

"Not again," she said. Soon her head hit the ceiling and her arms and legs pushed out through the windows and doors.

"I must eat something that will help me to shrink," Alice said.

With her long arm, she picked up a vegetable from the garden. As soon as she bit it, she began to shrink. Soon she was the right size, but she did not stop shrinking. When she stopped, she was VERY small.

The flowers outside were as tall as trees.

"What is *your* problem?" asked a strange voice.

Alice turned and saw a big blue caterpillar on top of a mushroom.

"I'm the wrong size," she began. But when she looked up, the Caterpillar was not there. It was in the air, and now it was a *butterfly*.

"Use the mushroom," cried the Butterfly before it flew away. "One side helps you to grow and the other side helps you to shrink."

Alice pulled off a piece of mushroom from each side.

Which one was right? She bit one of the pieces.

It was the right one – Alice started to grow again ... a LOT.

Very quickly she was taller than all the trees around her.

"What *are* you?" cried a bird. It was afraid of Alice.

"I'm just a little girl," she answered.

"LITTLE?" said the bird in surprise. It laughed at the idea.

Now Alice bit the other piece of mushroom. Seconds later she was smaller than the flowers again.

"Will I *ever* get this right?" Alice said.

Next, she licked the first piece of mushroom. Alice grew again, this time to the right size — *Alice size*.

Now she could look for the White Rabbit again. But where was he?

The forest was dark now, with signs everywhere — UP, DOWN, THIS WAY, BACK.

"Did you lose something?" asked *another* strange voice.

Alice looked up in surprise and saw a big smile up in the trees — no face or body, just a big, white smile in the night air. Then there were two yellow eyes above the smile, and then there was a face and body, too.

"You're a cat!" cried Alice.

The cat's big smile grew bigger. "I'm a Cheshire Cat," he said.

The Cheshire Cat pointed into the trees. "He went that way," he told Alice.

"Who?" Alice asked.

"The White Rabbit."

"He did?"

"*Who* did?" asked the cat.

"The White Rabbit!" cried Alice.

"*What* White Rabbit?"

Getting an answer from the Cheshire Cat was not easy.

But then he said, "To find the White Rabbit, you must ask the Mad Hatter and the March Hare." He pointed to a different part

The Mad Hatter and the March Hare sat at a long table with lots of plates and cups of tea.

"I'm sorry to come during your birthday party," said Alice.

"This isn't a birthday party!" cried the March Hare.

"This is an *un*-birthday party!" said the Mad Hatter. "You only have one birthday every year, but there are three hundred and sixty-four days that are NOT your birthday. They're your *un-birthdays*!"

"Today is my un-birthday, too!" said Alice.

It was a *very* strange tea party. Every few seconds the Mad Hatter shouted, "Clean cups!" Then they all had to move to a different chair and drink from a new cup.

Suddenly, a new guest ran into the party – the White Rabbit!

"I'm late!" he cried.

The Mad Hatter looked at the White Rabbit's watch. "You're *two days* late!"

The Mad Hatter and the March Hare broke the White Rabbit's watch and threw him out of the party.

Alice ran out of the garden after the rabbit, but she could not find him. She did not want to return to the Mad Hatter's party, so she walked into the dark forest.

There were lots of strange birds – birds with long necks and birds with long legs, birds with umbrellas for wings and birds with pencils for mouths.

Alice felt far from home – she just wanted to leave this place. She sat down and started to cry.

Something began to sing in one of the trees. Alice knew that voice.

"Oh, Cheshire Cat, it's you!"

Alice began to explain, "I'm not looking for the rabbit now. I just want to go home, but I can't find my way."

"If you want to go home, you must meet the Queen," said the cat.

He pulled down a stick and a big door opened in the tree. On the other side there was a sunny garden and a castle.

When she walked into the garden, she met three of the Queen's soldiers. They were busy with their paint brushes and a ladder.

"Why are you painting the white roses red?" asked Alice.

"We planted the white roses by mistake," said one of the soldiers. "The Queen likes *red* roses."

Alice was sure about one thing – these soldiers were all afraid of the Queen. She decided to help them with their job.

More soldiers came into the garden. A little animal ran to the front – it was the White Rabbit! Now Alice understood why the rabbit kept saying he was late. He was late for his job at the castle!

"The Queen!" the White Rabbit called just before she walked around the corner. The Queen was big and her face was not very friendly. The King followed her. His face *was* friendly and he was smaller than the rabbit!

When the Queen saw Alice, she asked, "Do you play croquet?"

"Yes," Alice answered.

The Queen wanted to play a game, but this was a strange kind of croquet. The ball was a little hedgehog, and the Queen used a flamingo to hit it. Alice tried to copy the Queen and play, but her flamingo and hedgehog did not help. They wanted the Queen to win because they were both afraid of her.

The Queen enjoyed the game at first, but soon she became angry.

"You cheated!" she shouted at Alice. Her face was red. "If I get angry, you lose your head!" The Queen shouted and shouted and then she fell down. Now she was VERY angry.

She pointed at Alice and shouted to her soldiers, "Off with her head!"

A little hand pulled at the Queen's dress. "Perhaps she can have a trial?" asked the King.

Lots of people were at the court to watch Alice's trial.

The Queen wanted to shout "Off with her head!" at the beginning, but first she had to listen to the March Hare.

"What do you know about this?" asked the White Rabbit.

"Nothing," said the March Hare.

Then all the people in the court had to listen to the Mad Hatter. He also knew nothing.

The Queen thought a little, and *then* she shouted,

"Off with her head!"

As soon as they heard this, all of the Queen's soldiers –
hundreds of them – flew toward Alice.

She did not want to lose her head! She jumped up and ran for
the door. The Queen and all her soldiers followed her, but Alice
did not stop. She ran through the gardens, through the forest,
by the Mad Hatter's table, and along an empty beach. The
Queen and all her soldiers were always behind her.

Alice ran and ran. She did not know where she was. There were clouds all around her.

But she did see one thing in front of her. It was the little door with the gold doorknob.

She tried to open the door, but it was not possible.

"OW!" cried the Doorknob.

"The Queen and all her soldiers are coming," said Alice. "I have to get out!"

"But you already *are* out," said the Doorknob.

Through the keyhole, Alice could see a girl asleep under a tree. It was *her*! It was *Alice*, with Dinah the cat in her arms.

"I'm *asleep*!" she cried in surprise.

She looked behind her. The Queen and all her soldiers were close now. The Mad Hatter and the March Hare were there, too. The Queen was still angry. She wanted Alice's head!

Alice turned back to the keyhole. "Alice!" she cried. "Wake up! Alice!"

"Alice, wake up!"

The voice was not Alice's now. It was her sister's.

Alice opened her eyes. She was back near the river.

Alice's sister still held her book open. "Tell me the answer, Alice," she said.

"Well the Caterpillar said ..." Alice stopped when she saw her sister's face.

Was it all a *dream*?

"It's time to go home for tea," said her sister.

Alice smiled. After her long, strange day, that was a good idea!

Before You Read

❶ Match the words and the pictures.

> flamingo   rose   hare   mushroom   hedgehog   caterpillar

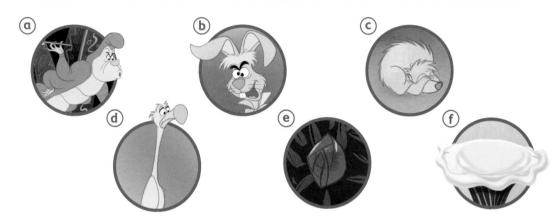

❷ Look at the picture on page 4 and answer the questions.

   a Where is Alice? What is strange about this picture?

   b What other strange things is she going to see?

After You Read

❶ Complete the sentences a–i with the verbs in the box.
Put the verbs in the past tense.

> make   fall   follow   grow   meet   shrink   wake up   want   play

   a Alice saw a white rabbit and _____ him.

   b Under the tree Alice _____ down a hole.

   c After Alice drank from the bottle, she _____ .

Activity page ②

d Alice _____ a sea with her tears.

e Alice _____ big again in the rabbit's house.

f Alice _____ a lot of very strange animals in the woods.

g Alice _____ a game of croquet with the Queen.

h The Queen _____ to cut off Alice's head.

i Alice _____ near the river.

2 **Match the pictures with the sentences a–h and the names 1–8.**

a He was always late.

b She was near the river with her sister.

c He became a butterfly.

d He was part of a little door.

e He wanted Alice to have a trial.

f He drank a lot of tea with the March Hare.

g At first Alice only saw his smile.

h The flamingo and hedgehog were afraid of her.

1 the Doorknob

2 the Caterpillar

3 the Queen

4 the King

5 Alice

6 the Cheshire Cat

7 the Mad Hatter

8 the White Rabbit

ALICE in WONDERLAND

A classic Disney story
re-told for young learners of Engl

Suddenly, Alice heard a new voice.

"I'm late!" said the voice nervously. "I'm late, for a very important date!"

Something ran by. It was a white rabbit.
He wore clothes and he held a big watch in one paw. "I'm late!" said the rabbit again.

Let's follow the rabbit to Wonderland!

Re-told by: Paul Shipton
Series Editor: Melanie Williams

Penguin Kids are simplified story books for children learning English.
MP3 audio is available at
www.penguinkidsaudio.cor

Penguin Kids has six levels:

Level	Headwords	CYLET
1	200	
2	400	
3	600	Starters
4	800	
5	**1000**	**Movers**
6	1200	

Teachers' factsheets: www.pearsonelt.com/penguinkids

ISBN 978-1-4082-8737-8

9 781408 287378 >

© Disney

Peter Pan

Comes to London

PENGUIN KIDS